Seven Animal
Adventure Stories

RETTY FORSTER

Contents

When stories are told in Sierra Leone folklore, the storyteller starts by saying "ILL" meaning that something has gone wrong. The listeners respond by saying "HOW"? Then the story unfolds to explain what went ILL.

The Lion The Pig and the Rabbit

ILL HOW?

Once upon a time the pig was taking his wife and family for a walk when they came across the Lion with its head caught in a trap.

"Please Mr Pig," said the Lion, "Set me free from this trap. I have been stuck here for five days with no food, and if I stay here much longer, I fear that I might die.

"I'm sorry," said Mr. Pig, "but I will not release you. You haven't eaten for such a long time that if I were to release you, you would want to eat up my whole family."

"What must you think of me Mr Pig? I would never be so ungrateful to someone who has helped to save my life. I promise you that I will not eat you or any member of your family if you release me." The lion, pleaded with the Pig to set him free.

"Well, since you've promised not to touch any of my family, show me what to do, and I shall release you," Said the Pig.

The Lion showed him how to pull a string that released his head from the trap that had held him captive for five days.

As soon as the lion was free, he roared very loudly, and then he said to the Pig "My, my, I'm spoiled for choice. Now which of you should I eat first?"

"But you promised that you wouldn't eat any of us" Said the surprised Pig.

"That just proves to me how stupid you are Pig. Did you really believe me? Can you really say that you expect me to let good food go because of one silly promise?" The Lion asked the Pig.

"But you cannot eat any of us, a promise is a promise, and it must be kept."

"You talk nonsense Pig," Said the Lion; "Now tell me which of your Piglets I should eat first."

"But you cannot eat my Piglets" said the Pig.

"In that case, shall I eat your wife first, or would you rather be first?"

By this time all of the little pigs had started to cry very, loudly.

Just then the Rabbit happened along on his afternoon walk.

"What is all the noise about?" He asked.

"We were on our walk when we came across the Lion stuck in a trap" explained the Pig "He asked me to free him but I refused at first, but after he promised not to harm me or my family, I released him. As soon as he was free, he turned on us, wanting to eat us up"

"Put yourself in my shoes" Said the lion to the rabbit "I haven't eaten in five days."

"What I don't understand," Said the Rabbit, "is how you were caught in the trap. I want you to show me where you were."

"I was right here," said the Lion and this rope was around my neck, and I was stuck."

"Put the rope round your neck and show me how you were stuck" said the Rabbit.

"It was like this," the Lion said, putting the trap over his head, and getting stuck again. At that point the Lion realized what had happened.

"I've helped you get rid of the threat of the Lion," Said the Rabbit to the Pig, "if you release him again, then you'll have to take the consequences". With that the Rabbit continued on his walk, followed by the Pig family, leaving the lion shouting out to them, begging for help.

How Dogs Came to Live in Houses

ILL HOW?

How dogs came to live in houses. All of the animals in the forest were very scared of the Fox. They would run if they saw him coming. One day all of the animals were chatting when the Dog said, "I don't know why you are all so scared of the Fox. I'm not scared of him at all. In fact, if all of you are here at this same time tomorrow, you will see me riding the Fox like a horse." "How do you plan to do that?" asked the Cat. "Just come along at this same time tomorrow and you will see" the Dog responded. All of the animals agreed to meet at the same spot the next day. The Dog went home and went straight to bed. He then called his eldest son and sent him with a message to the Fox. "Tell him I'm very ill, and that I cannot walk." He said. "I have to go to the Bush Doctor and I don't know how I will get to him." When the Fox heard of the Dog's illness, he came running to his bedside to see if he could help. "I would need to go to the Bush

Doctor tomorrow," said the Dog, "do you think you would be able to take me?" "Oh of course I would," replied the Fox, then he left and went home. The next day the Fox came back to see the Dog to take him to the Bush Doctor. He saw that the Dog was very weak, and couldn't walk, so he decided to carry him on his back. As they went through the forest they came across the other animals waiting at the appointed spot for Dog to prove his challenge. When they saw the Dog on the Fox's back, they started to laugh and fall about, saying "Dog said that he would ride the Fox like a horse, and true to his word, there he is riding the Fox like a horse." The Fox heard what the animals were saying and that made him very cross. He tried to put Dog down to attack, but the Dog was too fast for him. He jumped off the Fox's back and ran. He ran and ran till he came to the nearest town. He went into the first house he could see, and never returned to the forest again; and that is how Dogs came to live in houses.

The Cunning Rabbit Wins a Bride

ILL HOW?

Once upon a time, when the Tiger was the reigning king of the forest, it came a time when he decided that his daughter was of an age to be married. One day, the Tiger called the Fox, who was the town crier, and asked him to announce all round the kingdom, that his daughter was looking for a suitable husband, and that whosoever was interested in marrying the Tiger Princess would have to go through a test of endurance to prove their worthiness of the hand of the lovely Princess. The test of endurance was to be able to drink a mug of boiling water! On hearing about this challenge, all of the young male animals in the jungle came forward, in the hope that they would be able to win the hand of the princess in marriage. The Dog was the first animal to approach the king. He was very excited "Where is the mug of boiling water king?" he asked, "give it to me now so that I can drink it and be off with my bride. I shall be the envy of all of the other animals in this forest." The king's servant brought the Dog a mug of boiling water. As soon as the Dog set his paws on the hot mug, it burnt him, and he dropped it on the ground, spilling all of the hot water, then the Dog ran home screaming. The next animal to come for the challenge was the Duck. He approached the king saying, "Give me the water now king, everybody knows that Ducks love water. No doubt I'm soon to become your son-in-law." The servant brought the mug of boiling water and handed it to the duck that immediately put his beak into it. The boiling water went into the Duck's nose and burnt him. He dropped the mug and ran off quacking in pain. And so it happened that all of the young males of the jungle came to take up the challenge one after the other, and all of them failed miserably. Then one day the Rabbit approached the king saying, "I have come to marry your daughter king, and I'm ready to take the challenge." "O.K." said the king as he went to order his servant to bring in the mug of boiling water. Then the Rabbit said "but I will not take the challenge right now. If you don't mind king, I'd rather do it tomorrow afternoon, because I want to invite all of my family and my neighbors to come and cheer me on as I drink the boiling water. If I fail, they would be there to console me, and if I succeed, they would help me to celebrate." So the king agreed that the Rabbit would come back on the next day and face the challenge. The next day, the Rabbit arrived at the king's compound with his parents, his five sisters and seven brothers, his grandparents, his grand uncle and grandaunt, his ten cousins, and six of his neighbours. As soon as all of his relatives had settled down, the king ordered his servant to give Rabbit a mug of boiling water. Rabbit took the mug of boiling water, and walked up to his mother with it and said "Here it is ma, this is the mug of boiling water that I must drink if I am to gain the hand of the lovely Princess as my bride, can you see how hot it is? Please pray for me, pray so that I will be able to drink it." Then the Rabbit moved on to his father and said "Pa, this is the water I have to drink just because I want a wife. If I get through this challenge and win the hand of the lovely Princess, she will be an asset to the family, because she will be one more pair of hands to help us in the farm, so please pray for me, pray that I am able to drink this water." Then he moved on to his grandma, and emotional with tears in his eyes, he said, "Granny, You have come here today, because you love me, and I do so appreciate it. I am very happy to have your support, so pray for me pray for me Grandma, so that I will be able to drink this water." Then he moved on to his Grandfather and said "Grandpa, look at the steam coming from the water, since you have left your sick bed to come here to support me today, you must pray for me. You should pray so that I will be able to drink this water, and leave this compound a winner today." So the Rabbit moved on to each of his brothers, and each off his sisters, and all of his cousins and aunty and uncle, and his neighbours, and gave each one a little speech before asking them to pray for him. By the time he had been round to every member of his entourage, the water was cold enough for him to drink it comfortably. The king was very impressed as he watched the Rabbit drinking the water in the mug without even wincing. So the Rabbit won the hand of the beautiful Tiger Princess in marriage, and his family and friends danced and sang with him as he took his bride home.

How The Chameleon Got Its Colours

ILL HOW?

How the Chameleon got its colours. Once upon a time all the animals in the East African forest were like one big happy family. The Elephant was the king, and all the animals loved and respected him. One day he called a meeting of all of the animals. When they had all come together, the Elephant told them that he wanted to give them some beautiful colors, so that they would all look different and bright. All of the animals were very excited to hear this. They just couldn't wait to have different bright colors covering their hides. The Monkey said to the Lizard, "I'd like a bright blue on my back," and the Leopard thought that some bright yellow would make him a little bit more outstanding. As a matter of fact, the Leopard had ambitions of becoming the next king, and he felt that brighter colors would help to put him on the road to becoming the next king. As the animals chatted excitedly about the colors that they wanted, the king made an important announcement. "To be fair and be sure that only the most deserving receive the colors I have to share out, I propose that some sort of competition should take place amongst all of you, and the winner will receive the colors as his prize." The Elephant continued, "I am going to organize a race. Everybody will have a chance to participate in the race and the winner will take all of the colors and do with them as he wishes." The tortoise and the Chameleon didn't like the idea of a race, for they both happen to be very slow animals. "How could I stand a chance of winning against the likes of the Leopard? This is most unfair" Said the Tortoise to the king. "Not really" explained the Elephant. "If you use your intelligence, I'm sure you would find a way of racing with the faster animals." The Chameleon hearing what the king said, and worked out a plan. The race was planned for the next day. All of the animals lined up at the appointed place and time for the race to start. The Tortoise didn't bother to race, as he saw it as a waste of time. The Chameleon on the other hand, positioned himself very close to the Leopard. As soon as the king was about to start the race, the Chameleon climbed on to the Leopard's tail and made himself comfortable. The Leopard was didn't realize that he had extra weight on his tail. The race started and all of the animals were on their way. The winner was expected to sit on a special chair at the finishing post. The Leopard was the fastest animal in the forest, so he was first at the finishing post. As the Leopard went to sit on the chair, the Chameleon jumped off his tail and sat down before him, shouting "don't squash me, I was here before you." The Leopard looked round and saw the Chameleon. He couldn't believe his eyes, and neither could the other animals when they too got to the finish line. So the Chameleon was declared the winner of the race, and given all of the different colors. That's why where ever the Chameleon goes; he can take on the color of its surroundings.

Why Chickens Eat Cockroaches

ILL HOW?

Why chickens eat cockroaches Once upon a time, the Chicken and the Cockroach were very firm friends. That was at the time when all animals lived together as one big Family. One day the Chicken asked the Cockroach if they could come together and buy a farm. The Cockroach thought it was a wonderful idea, so they brought their monies together, and they soon bought a good size farm. Now, every day, they had to go to the Farm to weed, and water and plant seeds and tend the crops, and it was extremely hard work. Soon the Cockroach got fed up with it. He was very lazy anyway. One morning when the Chicken called for the Cockroach very early so they could get an early start at the farm, the Cockroach said that he wasn't feeling very well, so he wasn't able to go. The Chicken was very understanding. "If you're sick, you must rest till you feel better. Don't worry, I'll go to the farm and do the work, you just try and make yourself better" Said the Chicken to the Cockroach. So the Chicken went off to the farm alone. As soon as he was out of sight, the Cockroach got out of his sick bed, went out into the street and started to sing very loudly, for all of his neighbors to hear;

SONG:

I've fooled the chicken, you gossips

I said I was sick, but as you can see,

I'm not sick, all you gossips

Go tell him if you wish,

I just don't care,

I just don't care, you gossips!

He sang and danced all day, and when it was time for the Chicken to return home from the farm, the Cockroach went back to bed and covered himself up, pretending to be sick again. When the Chicken got home, he felt very sorry for the Cockroach, so he made him a hot drink, and tucked him into bed, telling him to try to get better soon.

The next day, the Chicken returned to the farm alone again. As soon as he was out of sight, the Cockroach got out of his sick bed, went out into the street and started dancing and singing his same song again, and very loudly too.

SONG:

I've fooled the chicken, you gossips

I said I was sick, but as you can see,

I'm not sick, all you gossips

Go tell him if you wish,

I just don't care,

I just don't care, you gossips!

When it was time for the Chicken to return home from the farm, the Cockroach went back to bed, and pretended to be sick again. The Chicken hurried home to make him a hot drink and tuck him into bed, telling him to take good care of himself. The next day, as soon as the Chicken left for the farm, the Cockroach was out of bed, in the Street, singing very loudly and dancing again. This time the Fly decided to do something about it. He went to the farm and asked the Chicken to come with him urgently. "Has something bad happened to Cockroach, is he dead?" Asked the Chicken anxiously. "Just come with me", said the Fly, "you will soon be able to judge for yourself." It was a very worried Chicken that followed the Fly home. They arrived in good time for the Chicken to see with his own eyes as the Cockroach danced and sang;

SONG:

I've fooled the chicken, you gossips

I said I was sick, but as you can see,

I'm not sick, all you gossips

Go tell him if you wish,

I just don't care,

I just don't care, you gossips!

When the Chicken saw this, he was so annoyed, that he just went up to the Cockroach and ate him up. Ever since that day, every time the chicken sees a Cockroach, he eats it up.

Why Chickens Scratch The Ground

ILL HOW?

Why chickens scratch the ground. The Hen and the Hawk were once engaged to be married. The Hawk gave the Hen a beautiful ring that she wore on her toe. The Hawk told the hen that he was not very happy to see the ring on her toe. "You will lose that ring on your toe, keep it somewhere else that is safe," he told the Hen. "I'll not lose it" the Hen replied, "I'm always keeping my eye on it." "I think that you are being stubborn," said the Hawk "I know what I am talking about. You are moving about all of the time, you won't know when it drops off your toe." "Oh, you only like to fuss," replied the Hen, "I'm a very careful chicken, and I know that I will not lose the ring." "Well, since you are so confident, I shall say no more," Said the Hawk. "But keep this in mind, if you lose that ring, make sure that I never get to hear about it, because if I do, I shall eat you and the rest of your family. A word to the wise is sufficient. Now I the matter closed." One day, the

Hen was digging through a haystack with her beak looking for grain when the ring slipped quietly off her toe. She didn't even notice that she had lost the ring. In the evening, she was supposed to visit the Hawk. She was just about ready to go out when she realized that the ring was no longer on her toe. She ran out into the yard, and started to look for it. She searched everywhere, but she couldn't find it. It was getting rather late, and the Hawk was waiting for her. "Maybe he won't notice that the ring is not on my toe," She said to herself. "I'll take the chance and go to see him." So the Hen went to see the Hawk without the ring on her toe. As soon as the Hawk saw her, before even saying hello he asked, "Where is my ring?" "I've ere err I've lo... lo. Left it at home" the Hen stuttered out very nervously. "Well, you'll have to go home and get it," said the Hawk, "because I don't like seeing you without it besides, if you have lost it, you know what will happen." "Yes . . . Yes. I. .I. Know" replied the Hen "I'll just.... err... err...run home and get it. I won't be long." And as she said that, she went away to search through the haystack for the ring. She couldn't find it, and till this day the chicken goes around digging theground looking for her engagement ring. And since that day, whenever the Hawk sees a chicken family it tries to eat it up.

The Greedy Spider

ILL HOW?

Spider was a very greedy animal. Every time there was a party or a banquet in the land of the animals, the spider would be present, and he would eat the most. So it happened that there were four different banquets planned for the same day, and the spider had been invited to all four. As everybody knows, it is physically impossible to be at four different places at the same time, and as it happened, all of these banquets were taking place in four completely different directions. They were not even remotely near each other, but the spider was determined to attend all of the four occasions so he devised a plan. The spider had four children, so he called all four of them to a meeting, and asked each one to attend one each of the banquets. Then he gave each one of them one end of a piece of string, he tied the other end of each of the pieces of strings around his waist, and stayed at home. He sent his children off with instructions to pull on the string as soon as good food was being served at the banquet they were at, and he would know which one to attend, and get there in time to eat. What the spider did not realize was that all four banquets would be serving food at exactly the same time. Each child according to their instructions, pulled at the string as soon as the food was being served, and suddenly the spider found himself being pulled into four different directions at the same time, and he soon realized that he was in trouble. Though the spider couldn't attend all of the banquets, he did learn a very important lesson, and that is being greedy is a very bad thing. Since that day, the spider has always had a tiny waist.